Surprise Pancakes for Mum

GW01003535

by Anne Giulieri

illustrated by Susy Boyer

"Alex," said Dad.
"Where is Mum?"

MILK

"She is in bed," said Alex.
"I can cook pancakes
for Mum.
It is a **big** surprise!"

"I can cook
the pancakes, too," said Dad.

Dad and Alex
cooked the pancakes.

"Mum can eat this pancake," said Dad.

"She can eat this banana, too," said Alex. "It can go on the pancake."

"Oh, no!" said Alex.
"Where is Mum?
She is not in bed."

"Alex," said Mum.
"Where are you?"

Alex jumped up!
Dad jumped up, too!

“**Surprise!**” shouted Alex.

“**Surprise!**” shouted Dad.

"Here is a surprise pancake for you," said Alex.